The Sapling

PRAISE FOR *STORYSHARES*

"One of the brightest innovators and game-changers in the education industry."
– Forbes

"Your success in applying research-validated practices to promote literacy serves as a valuable model for other organizations seeking to create evidence-based literacy programs."

- Library of Congress

"We need powerful social and educational innovation, and Storyshares is breaking new ground. The organization addresses critical problems facing our students and teachers. I am excited about the strategies it brings to the collective work of making sure every student has an equal chance in life."
– Teach For America

"Around the world, this is one of the up-and-coming trailblazers changing the landscape of literacy and education."
- International Literacy Association

"It's the perfect idea. There's really nothing like this. I mean wow, this will be a wonderful experience for young people."   - Andrea Davis Pinkney, Executive Director, Scholastic

"Reading for meaning opens opportunities for a lifetime of learning. Providing emerging readers with engaging texts that are designed to offer both challenges and support for each individual will improve their lives for years to come. Storyshares is a wonderful start."
- David Rose, Co-founder of CAST & UDL

The Sapling

Roan McAuley

STORYSHARES

New York. Boston. Philadelphia

Storyshares

Story Share, Inc.
24 N. Bryn Mawr Avenue #340
Bryn Mawr, PA 19010-3304
www.storyshares.org

Inspiring reading with a new kind of book.

Interest Level: High School
Grade Level Equivalent: 3.9

9798885977500

Book design by Storyshares

Printed in the United States of America

Storyshares Presents

1

I had trouble writing a poem this morning. Something about the way I woke up just seemed off for some reason.

Maybe it was the larger-than-usual gap in the curtains. It had woken me up a few minutes earlier than my usual alarm. Maybe it was something else. It made me feel like writing something a little deeper than usual.

Anyhow, what I eventually came up with was this:

There are times in life you'd rather stay down,

Surrender instead of getting back on your feet.

But in the end, even the act of moving on

Is one of life's greatest challenges, beat.

As I finished writing the last word on the notebook page, my bedroom clock silently called. I turned around in my chair. 6:59.

I felt myself quickly get up from my seated position, grab my backpack, and head out my bedroom door. I closed it behind me a little too quickly and made it slam.

Right on cue, the voice of my mother rang through the house. It seemed to come from both nowhere and everywhere. "Colin! Stop slamming doors! Don't—"

"Sorry!" I called back, cutting her off.

I didn't stick around for any possible response. I had already walked through the main hallway and out the front door. I made sure to close it slowly, softly letting the handle click back into place as I let go.

The air was cold, almost windy in its chilly stillness. I felt myself jolt fully awake. A deep exhale escaped my mouth. I grabbed my backpack straps comfortingly before I set out.

Everything everywhere was green and growing. That was, of course, the way it should be. There hadn't been any snow this winter. Instead, everything had just been dead and bare for about four months. Even the pines had lost most of their needles.

Now, it was finally beginning to feel like March for a change. Almost all the trees and leaves wore layers of green that made the walk to school actually enjoyable for once.

In what felt like a blink of an eye, I was already standing in front of Olive Pass High School. All of the trees here were still leafless, waiting for some growth to happen. If it was going to come at all.

Just like any other day, I walked up to the A building. That was where the main auditorium and gym were. I needed to get to the B building, which stood right behind it.

There were people everywhere. Walking, chatting, laughing. Doing what high schoolers couldn't seem to stop doing. The noises of dozens of other students fell on everything like a downpour of endless rain.

I tried to move as quickly as I could through the crowds, dodging someone running past here and moving around a clump of laughing kids there.

I tried not to pay too much attention to any of the people. Although most of them hopefully didn't even know my name, the chance for an unpleasant meeting was still there.

I spotted Ben Carson and Jack Evens among their large group of athletic friends. They were just hanging around. Some of them punched each other in what was clearly meant to be a friendly move. The last thing I wanted was for that to happen to me, friendly or not.

Soon enough, I made it all the way to B140, Mrs. Allen's room. The hallway here was mostly deserted. Class didn't start for — I looked up at a nearby clock — about six minutes or so.

I grabbed the handle for the classroom door and turned it. Or rather, tried to. A small moment of surprise washed over me as I quickly realized that the classroom was locked. Mrs. Allen never locked her room before class. What could possibly cause this break in routine?

I looked inside through the small glass window on the door. I saw a dark space with no one in it. How odd.

Class started in five minutes. Was Mrs. Allen late? Would class be canceled?

"Hup, excuse me," a voice said.

I turned around and saw a strange man. He wore a casual plaid shirt and khaki pants. He wore glasses, had wavy hair almost to his shoulders, and looked in his late twenties or so.

I instinctively backed away from the door.

"You in Mrs. Allen's class?" the man asked, as he pulled out a key and unlocked the classroom.

Yes.

And then, realizing I hadn't actually given a physical or verbal answer, I quickly nodded.

"Nice," the man said.

He stood back from the now open classroom door and gestured for me to enter. I did so, a little on edge.

Is Mrs. Allen sick, or something? I said it a couple times inside my head before speaking.

Is Mrs. Allen sick, or something?

"Is Mrs. Allen sick, or something?"

"Something like that," the man said. He walked over and switched on the lights. "Or I think she might just be taking the day off. I'd have to read her notes again..."

A loud, clanging noise suddenly sounded. It signaled the five-minute mark until class officially started for the day. Even though it was a broadcast, the school still used a recording of one of those old-style metallic bells. You could almost hear the rust mixed in with the grainy quality of the recording.

I sat down in my seat, the one in the front corner, close to both the door and the front of the classroom. Since I'd been the first person to show up on the first day of school, Mrs. Allen had let me choose my seat. I'd refused to give it up for the entire school year so far, guarding it carefully. Not that I'd had any competition, or anything.

"Hey, what's your name?" the man asked. "Might as well mark you off on the attendance now, since you're here."

"Uh..." For a moment, my mouth seemed to lag. I hadn't expected to be asked something so directly. "Colin," I heard myself say.

"Richardson?" the man said, reading a piece of paper that must have been the attendance form.

"Yeah," I said.

The sound of the door swinging open started the slow trickle of other students into the class. I tried to look wrapped up in my own thoughts. But really, I was focused on the people as they entered the room, passed my desk, and sat down in their own seats in the classroom.

None of them interacted with me negatively, or at all, for which I was grateful. It was too early in the morning for anything like that.

Before long, the bell rang again. Now the classroom was filled with students.

"Hey, Mrs. Allen's absent today, so I'll be filling in for the day. You can call me Mr. McKilven, or just Mr. M." He wrote his name on the whiteboard with a faded expo marker. "So, this is AP English, right? Let's see here..." He read a piece of paper for a moment. "All right, so it looks like you're supposed to finish analyzing the Robert Frost poem you've been working on. Then you can work on any other work for this class for the rest of the period."

Everyone else started talking to everyone else. Some were working on the assignment. Most weren't.

I sat back in my chair. I had already finished the poem worksheet, and I didn't have any other work. I guess anyone else would've considered it a stroke of luck.

"You all good?" said Mr. M, approaching my desk.

"Yeah, yeah," I heard myself say. "I just, uh, already finished all the work, and so, you know..."

"Ah, I see." Mr. M gave a kindly grin.

I wondered what kind of circumstances would lead someone to become a high school substitute teacher and still keep a cheerful outlook on life.

"Well, relax, chill," he said. "You're all set."

Mr. M then walked back to the front of the room, sat down, and began reading a paperback novel. It was called *The Interesting* Something Or Other. I couldn't read the whole title from where I was, as his hand blocked most of the cover.

"Hey, did you finish?"

The voice came from my left, which was unusual. My head whirled around in that direction.

"What'd you get for number five?"

It was Abigail Eatons, who sat at the desk directly next to me. Today, she was wearing a lime green sweater that I couldn't help but think was a little too close to neon. Her brilliant green eyes looked about as acidic as her sweater.

I suddenly realized I hadn't answered her question.

"Uh," I managed to say. "I don't have it out, let me—" I reached into my backpack, flipping through papers until I found the assignment. "Here." I slid the assignment across my desk.

Abigail looked surprised, like she hadn't been asking me at all. "Oh, I wasn't..."

I suddenly felt what it must feel like for a houseplant to wilt.

But she leaned over to read the answer, squinting. After a moment, she said, "Cool. Thanks."

And just like that, the conversation ended.

The silence that filled the following moment suddenly became overwhelming. It felt like I was in the vacuum of space, where no sound is ever heard.

Was there something else that was supposed to happen? Why did the mood feel so... so lacking, like there was something important missing?

2

I checked my watch as I approached the park. 3:11. It was pretty good timing. I'd walked faster than usual.

Everything was still warm shades of green and brown, along with the dirt path that went into the forest. The painted green sign, which read "Olive Ridge Park," had a light blue outline that made it stand out from everything else. But it somehow seemed to fit in with its surroundings.

I took my usual route, staying on the main path until I reached the first bench. Then I went onto the left path up the hill.

Usually I took in the beauty of my surroundings as much as I could, but today I found my mind wandering somewhere else. It was in a place of vague feelings that couldn't really be put into specific words. The kind of feelings that drive one to wander without really knowing why.

Before I knew it, I found myself at the stump. I had to stop and look at it for a moment before realizing I had already walked this far. What was up with me today? Why was I so... out of the world and inside my head?

The stump was from an ancient cedar, cut down long ago. It was about six feet wide, a deep brown, and had been the largest tree around when it had still been a tree. Time had weathered it down, and now all of its edges were relatively smooth. A small section of it was taller than the rest, creating a small plateau on its left side. That was where I usually liked to sit.

I slid my backpack off, dropped it at the base of the stump, then sat down on the raised part of it.

There was something else on the stump, which was another reason I always liked sitting there. Out of the ancient remnant, a small sapling was growing up through the wood.

It was only about a foot high, and had only two real branches. But it was already growing little needles of its own. It was so small and innocent, so beautiful in an untouched sort of way, like the first buds on a tree in spring. Except this cycle had taken years to restart anew.

I turned away from the tree and looked out over the forest. The air wasn't very cold, but I sat back and put my legs on the stump, bent so they were standing directly in front of me. I wrapped my arms around them. I sat there for a moment, simply watching the trees waving back and forth in the gentle wind.

Suddenly, all of the gorgeous greenery glowing in the afternoon light turned into a backdrop. A strange stillness and quiet seemed to surround me. It wasn't a feeling I'd ever felt before, or at least not often enough to clearly remember it.

I was suddenly aware of how isolated I was, in that moment.

I was the only person there for a mile or so, at least. But... there was something else, too.

I was the only person who knew I was there.

I frowned as I tried to think. Being alone couldn't be the problem. It couldn't be. I was alone all the time, after all. Even when I was surrounded by other people. And I never felt... lonely. Why would I now? There was no reason I should. I had always gotten by fine by myself.

I clutched my legs a little tighter and rested my chin on my knees, looking over the greens of the trees.

I woke up earlier than my alarm, and was able to turn it off before it blared. I lay there for a moment, looking up at the dimly-lit ceiling from under my blanket. I wasn't sure what was keeping me from getting up.

After an instant and an eternity, I pulled my covers off in a sweeping motion and slid out of bed. After getting dressed, I sat down at my desk, racking my brain for a muse. I wrote down the poem, a small part of me unsure of what it really meant:

Sometimes life is like a gentle wind,

Sometimes sharp, sometimes cold & chill.

And sometimes we chose to keep walking,

Knowing that whatever happens, will.

I turned and looked at my bedroom clock. 7:01.

I quickly grabbed my backpack from the foot of my bed. I opened my door, passed through it, and shut it closed.

"Colin! Don't slam doors! Don't even—" my mother called.

"Sorry!" I answered.

My face felt the chill morning air as I walked out the front door. I grabbed onto my backpack straps, inhaled a deep breath of the cold, then set out across the front lawn.

I walked across the street to the sidewalk, the firm cement feeling stiff beneath my feet. I walked up to the front of Olive Pass High School, the brick buildings almost sinking into the ground. I walked through the chattering crowds to the B building, where people ran and shouted and talked. I walked down the hallway to B140, where the only noise was my own footsteps. I walked up to the door, which was open.

The classroom lights were already on. Mr. M was already inside, sitting down at the desk.

"Oh, hey, Colin!" he said, looking up from his novel. "Early again, huh?"

"Uh, yeah," I heard myself say, nodding at the same time.

"Well, it's good to be punctual, you know. Good to know how to prioritize yourself," Mr. M said.

I didn't quite know how to respond to this, let alone speak an answer out loud. Mr. M looked back at his page and quiet came to the room once more. The task at hand returned to my mind.

Hello.

No, that's not it.

Hello.

Ah, not quite.

Hello.

Soon enough, the clang of the morning bell gave a five-minute warning to the several thousand teenagers nearby. Students began to file into the classroom.

Abigail was one of the last stragglers to enter through the door. As the final bell announced the start of the morning, she quickly sat down in her seat.

"Hello," I said.

"Oh, uh... Hi," she said. Then she turned away to fish something out of her backpack.

She didn't turn back around in my direction. Instead she started chatting with the person in the next seat over, Vanessa Toler. From what I'd heard, the two of them were in the same core friend group. Still, the feeling in my mind wasn't exactly pleasant. It was like I'd just taken too big of a bite of something sour and then tried to swallow it anyway.

"All right!" Mr. M called across the classroom, silencing most of the side conversations. "As you can see, Mrs. Allen is still out, so I'm still here. Today, you guys are going to..."

"Hey, we still on for after school?" whispered Vanessa.

"Yeah, Ben doesn't have practice today," said Abigail.

"After school?" The words fell out of my mouth before I could stop them.

Immediately I knew I'd made a mistake. Of course I hadn't been included in the conversation.

Abigail and Vanessa both looked at me, which was a new experience.

"Oh," said Abigail, hesitantly. "Well—"

"Sorry," I said, reflexively.

"No, no," said Abigail in a way that seemed reassuring. Hopefully it was, anyway. "You just... don't usually talk."

It was hard to tell whether her view of me was positive or not.

"We're just gonna, you know, hang out behind the gym after school. That's all," Abigail said.

She turned away and looked to the front of the classroom. After all, there was still an actively speaking teacher.

A strange force seemed to tug my spirits upward. Had that been... an invitation? All the negative thoughts seemed to leave me.

Something to look forward to at last.

3

"So... who are you again?"

"Uh... Colin." Every time I said it I felt a little less sure, like even my name could be damaged by the awkwardness.

"Ben, knock it off," said Abigail in clipped tones. But she quickly fell silent herself.

Vanessa, who had been scrolling through her phone for the past five minutes, looked up. Upon making unexpected eye contact with me, she quickly looked back to the screen.

Jack was leaning against the building's wall. He slid down it until he was sitting down and mindlessly stared off into the distance. He only looked once at me before going back to his faraway focus.

None of them spoke to each other. Or to me.

Clearly, these people needed some more excitement in their lives.

What are you guys doing tomorrow?

I mean, the scenario was a little disappointing, to say the least. But it was something. Maybe I was on my way to turning this whole thing around. The feeling of being around other people like this was overwhelming, exciting in a strange way.

What are you guys doing tomorrow?

I checked my watch. 3:09. I guessed I'd be a few minutes late getting to the park.

What are you guys doing tomorrow?

"What are, uh, you guys doing tomorrow?" I said, pursing my lips afterward.

There was a moment of awkward silence in the following few moments. Maybe they were all just trying to think.

"I mean, the mall," said Abigail, not looking at me, "But—"

Vanessa suddenly kicked her hard in the shin, clearly trying and failing to be subtle. It was odd, to say the least. I couldn't help but flinch at the action. It looked like it hurt, too.

"The mall?" The question came out of my mouth, even though I'd meant it as a statement.

I nodded to move past it, then looked at my watch again as I backed away. It wasn't supposed to rain until later, so I'd spend some good time in the forest before the storm came.

The Sapling

4

The sapling seemed to sense the oncoming weather. It was barely vibrating, almost twitching in the gentle, wet wind. The rain would be arriving soon.

I sat on the stump, looking at the sapling rather than the scenery. I wondered if it might get damaged in the rain, if it could get flooded somehow. But I rejected the idea. After all, it had survived this far, hadn't it? Surely it would last for years to come, despite the weather that poured down upon it.

Still, the little tree looked so small, so delicate. As if it was just waiting to see what kind of dangers the world would throw at it.

5

I woke up late, since it wasn't a school day. Maybe that's why I couldn't think of a poem to write. Maybe it was just because it was Saturday.

I rolled out of bed, saw the clock, and squinted at it. It was always a little disorienting to wake up at 8:30 in the morning after getting up so early during the week.

The Mall.

Instantly, I remembered the events of the day before. The Mall.

I sat down at my desk, pushing aside my poetry notebook and opening my laptop. I typed into the search engine until I found out what time the Olive Pass Mall opened.

9:00 AM.

I'd be able to get there just in time.

6

The earliness of the hour meant that the normally crowded mall was almost deserted, especially since it was still all wet outside from the night's rain. There were a few scattered people walking back and forth between the different stores, and sometimes groups of two or three. But for the most part, the large, empty space was just that: empty.

It gave me a pleasant and calming feeling, being there in that time and setting. Like that feeling you get at airports in the middle of the night. So much so that I almost forgot why I'd bothered going there in the first place.

I had to wait for some time before I saw them. It was almost 11:00 before I spotted them walking through the main courtyard.

So, where are we going first?

All four of them looked surprised to see me there. Ben's eyebrows were frowning and Vanessa's mouth had gone limp, almost like an expression of disgust.

So, where are we going first?

I felt more confident seeing them all there, and my vocal cords seemed to agree. I approached them, straightened up, and said, "So, where are we going first?"

All four of them gave nervous glances at each other. I guess they hadn't thought of that beforehand.

I stood there for a moment, waiting for one of them to say something, but no one did.

I had always thought — or been told by others — that I was quiet. Quiet. As in, didn't speak as much as other people did. However, a small seed of curiosity began to sprout in my mind as I watched these four regular teenagers at a loss for words.

Suddenly, an idea came to me: maybe everyone is Quiet in one way or another, and I just hadn't noticed until now. The thought gave me a strange feeling. It was difficult to describe. Like I wasn't quite so out of place in the world.

Vanessa started walking away, and the other three soon followed her.

I thought about asking where she'd decided to go, but I didn't. We'd get there eventually. I walked up behind the other three, feeling an excited eagerness for the adventure.

Only Abigail gave me a glance to check if I was still there. I smiled in response, or tried to anyway. It sort of became a half smile, half nod that probably communicated very little at all. She turned her head to face forward again.

It was Jack who broke the silence. "So... uh, you think Coach will be alright for the game?"

The conversation was clearly directed toward Ben. He answered with, "I dunno, probably. It hasn't been canceled, so it'll probably be fine."

"Who are you guys playing again?" Abigail asked.

"South Lake," said Jack. "Apparently their lead pitcher has an ERA of 2.5."

"Pfft. No way," said Ben. "Where'd you hear that?"

The football — baseball? — conversation went on as we passed rows of department stores and shops. We seemed to be headed in no particular direction. Vanessa was still leading the way, half looking at her phone.

The mall was beginning to be more crowded now. It would've been harder to get through the crowds of people if I hadn't been following behind Ben, Jack, and Abigail. I tuned back in to their conversation.

"Look, I just don't believe that he could have that low of an ERA," Ben was saying.

"Believe me," said Jack. "When has Matthew ever been wrong?"

When's the game?

"Um," said Abigail, "I'm pretty sure he failed every single one of his Algebra tests."

When's the game?

"Hey," said Jack, "I'm pretty sure I failed every single of my Algebra tests."

"When's the—" I started to say, but Ben cut me off.

"No way a high schooler has an ERA of 2.5. It's just not possible." Ben snorted, as if the whole idea was completely ridiculous.

I stayed silent, not bothering to repeat what I'd failed to say. I guess they hadn't heard.

By now, we'd circled through the entire mall and ended up back where we had started from in the first place. The food court was now bustling with shoppers and lunch-goers alike. It was far from the peaceful atmosphere I'd been waiting in earlier that morning.

"Y'all hungry?" asked Abigail.

I think so.

"Oh yeah," said Jack.

I think so.

"Yup," said Ben.

"I think—" I tried to say.

"Well, where do you wanna eat?" Jack asked.

"How about Chipotle?" said Vanessa, speaking for the first time since I'd arrived.

"Sure," said Ben, sounding excited. "I haven't eaten since breakfast."

"You didn't eat breakfast," said Abigail.

"Exactly," Ben said. He led the way to the small Chipotle shop on the far end of the food court.

I hadn't thought to bring any money, so I couldn't get anything. I stood a few feet away as the four of them ordered. It took a while, since there was already a slow-moving line. I had the idea of doing something, but didn't quite know what to do.

Once they'd all gotten their food, I followed them to a small table in the middle of a sea of other tables that looked just like it. The table sat four people, and I was left standing awkwardly as they all sat down.

"Um," I said, not quite knowing what I was going to say after that.

"Ben, where are your manners?" asked Jack, in a voice that was a blend of honey and vinegar. "Go get the weirdo a chair."

Ben was in the middle of a large bite of a taco. He said, in a muffled tone, "Fine."

I stood there for a few more moments, waiting for Ben to finish his bite. I didn't want to get a chair for myself now that the suggestion had been made. Ben stood up, grabbed a chair from an empty table, and plopped it down.

Slowly, I sat down.

The rest of lunch went by as I sat there. I felt more isolated than I'd ever felt before while I sat in the middle of the crowds of people walking, talking, and enjoying each other's company. The rest of the world seemed to be pressing down on me, trying to drown me in an atmosphere too thick to breathe. And there was nothing I could do about it except wait and hope this wasn't the new normal.

"Colin, you coming?"

It was Abigail, who had been the last to get up from the table. She looked concerned. It immediately blew away all of the fog in my mind.

"Yeah, yeah." I got up from the table and tried to push the fifth chair into it before giving up and following the group.

Probably because everyone had just eaten lunch, the four of them were walking at a slower pace than before. I couldn't help but notice that we hadn't actually gone into any of the stores. That is, after all, what malls are made up of.

There wasn't any conversation, either. The five of us simply kept walking without saying a word.

After a while, our speed slowed to a stop, standing in an empty hallway. Several lower-tier stores surrounded us. Only a few other people were around.

"Did you hear about Jessica Fletcher?" Vanessa asked Abigail.

"Hmm? What about?" Abigail asked.

"Hey," said Jack, nudging Ben in the shoulder. "I dare you to eat that." He pointed to a nearby banister, where a chewed-up wad of gum sat.

"Pfft," Ben said. "I'll pass."

"You eat it then," Jack said, and nodded at me.

What?

This was the first time that Jack had acknowledged my existence, let alone spoken directly to me. After the bittersweet moment of accomplishment, I realized what he'd asked.

I looked down at the piece of gum. It was faded orange and wrinkled, like a dehydrated brain. It was falling slightly to the side of the railing as a result of its own weight. It was small, about the size of a pill, but completely unappetizing.

My lack of an answer seemed to be taken as encouragement.

Jack started to chant. "Eat it, eat it, eat it..."

I looked at the piece of gum. Was it worth it for the sake of being included?

Getting the moment over as quickly as possible, I grabbed the piece, unstuck it from the banister, and popped it into my mouth. The texture wasn't terrible but the taste was awful, like lint had been made into an ice cream flavor.

"Don't actually eat it, you idiot!" Ben clenched his hand into a fist and slapped it against my back.

I choked on the gum and violently spit it out onto the floor, where it stuck like a suction dart.

Abigail and Vanessa, who had been wrapped up in their own conversation, made noises of alarm and disgust.

Jack looked stunned. "Wow. I didn't think you'd actually do that. Good job, then." He grinned and punched me in the right shoulder.

It stung like nobody's business, and was even worse than the gum. It almost felt like an electric shock that rippled through my entire torso. Nobody else seemed to be fazed at my sudden physical pain.

"Well, where do we go now?" Vanessa asked.

"I dunno," said Jack. "Somewhere."

I needed a breath of fresh air.

"I know a place," I felt myself say as I rubbed my shoulder.

The Sapling

7

The clean, cool breeze filled my lungs. I couldn't help but walk at my usual pace, even though my arm was still tingling from the supposedly friendly punch. Several times I had to stop and listen to find out if everyone else was still behind me, hearing footsteps a moment or so later.

The trees seemed duller today. That was probably just because of the overcast clouds that drifted above, like a shadow of doubt upon the face of the world. Not on me, though. For once, I knew everything was better than it should be.

Soon, we reached the stump. As a habit, I climbed on top of it and sat down.

The sapling stood where it always did, in its little place in the center of the stump. For some reason it seemed smaller today, almost as if it was a little more shy than usual. I smiled at it, as if to cheer it up. It didn't react, of course, but I felt a little better for having done it.

"What is this place?" Abigail asked.

"I dunno. Just like to come here sometimes," I heard myself say. "Look over all the trees."

Out of the corner of my eye, I saw Jack kick his foot against one of the trees, clearly bored. He seemed to always be bored in some way, no matter what was going on. He'd probably scoff and yawn if the Entertainer himself showed up.

I turned away and looked out over the green of the trees. All of them were blowing a little more actively in the wind, which had turned into something a little more stormy. I hadn't thought to check and see if there was any rain in the forecast. For some reason, I didn't worry about the possibility of a storm. If it happened, I knew I'd get through it.

"It's too cold," said Vanessa's voice from somewhere behind me.

"We should've stayed at the mall," Ben said, bordering on a complaint.

"Yeah," agreed Jack. His footsteps made me turn around. "There's nothing even out here."

Everything in his voice said "I'm Bored."

Then, time seemed to slow until it almost stopped. In one moment that lasted an eternity, I sat stuck to the stump like gum on a banister. I watched, helpless, as Jack, casual as ever, walked over and reached out...

And ripped the sapling out of the stump with his bare hand.

A shrieking scream filled the air. It took me a moment to realize that it was my own, inside my head.

"I'm outta here," said Jack, dropping the uprooted sapling.

It softly began to fall downwards.

It floated like a leaf in an autumn wind. Then it collided with the dirt, its smallest branch splayed to one side. Many of its needles had fallen off and made their own journeys to the ground. They now surrounded the injured sapling, which lay there, helpless.

Everyone said their own small goodbyes as Jack began to walk away. I thought about saying something, too. I thought about shouting. I thought about cursing under my breath or at the top of my lungs.

Then I stopped thinking at all.

I stood up and walked over to Jack, aimed for his crotch, and kicked as hard as I could.

8

I didn't fall asleep until after 11:30 that night, so I didn't wake up until about 10:00 the next morning. Not that it made a difference.

I looked around my bedroom, which had somehow gotten more cluttered and chaotic than it had been the night before. The curtains, which had been quickly shut the night before, were bunched up in places. They left clear gaps where I could see bits of the outside.

My backpack sat face-down in the middle of the floor in silent misery, its contents jumbled and spilling out of the main pocket. The covers on my bed had been tossed and turned in every direction. The sheet was bunched up near the wall and the blanket was falling off the other side.

I didn't want to get up at all. But my own physical discomfort gave me little choice. Clearly, being asleep for almost ten hours had done little. So much for "you'll feel better in the morning."

I looked at the clock again. 10:02. Was this how time was going to pass from now on? Slow, tedious, and dragging along?

I lay down in the middle of my floor next to my backpack, closed my eyes, and let out an exhale I didn't realize I was holding in. Right now, time could go as slow as it wanted to.

9

My expression stayed as tightly closed as possible as I walked toward the stadium. My elbows were stiff and my teeth were almost grinding against each other.

I had only a vague idea of what I wanted to say, but I knew beyond anything else that I wanted to say it. I would walk right up to the four of them, look each and every one of them in the eye, and say, "You're all a-holes."

The baseball field was already scattered with people. All of them wore uniforms of white and green, which were the school colors. On the opposite side of the field was a group in purple and orange, which I assumed were from South Lake High.

I walked up behind the rattling metal bleachers and scanned my surroundings. I had wondered if I would even find the four of them together. I was doubtful that they would all be in the same place at the same time. But I was lucky.

Just behind the metal seats, in front of a cluster of pines, I saw them all. Abigail, Ben, Jack, and Vanessa. They were talking to each other in what seemed like a not-so-casual way. I approached them from the direction of the trees.

Jack sounded angry. I stood behind one of the trees, choosing to listen and watch before I entered.

"What were you even thinking?" Jack was asking. "Letting that freak tag along?"

Abigail seemed upset. "I dunno!"

A flicker of hope rose in me, like the spark that would soon start a fire.

"I— I just felt sorry for him!" Abigail said. "He seemed like he just needed a friend, even if he was a weirdo. I didn't know he'd be all like that!"

The spark died.

I felt something drain out of my mind, like a phone must feel when you unplug it from the charger. I felt myself stand up a little straighter as I kept watching, not bothering to listen. I heard a voice inside, one that I hadn't heard in some time.

Walk away.

I let out a breath. And looked at the four of them one last time. Jack, Vanessa, Ben, and Abigail, all standing there.

Then I walked away.

10

The Sapling

The cool, wet wind blew against my face, giving me a gentle chill. I looked out over the view of green trees, softly swaying in the breeze.

I hugged my bent legs and rested my chin on my knees as I sat still on the stump, breathing in the cold air. But it was a good kind of cold, one that settles you down and grounds you to the earth.

I had propped up what was left of the sapling against the stump, facing the landscape. I had tried to replant it, but it was too far gone. It sat there, injured, looking out over its surroundings. Nothing and no one would hurt it any more.

I took a deep breath in, then slowly let it out.

There are times in life you'd rather stay down, surrender instead of getting back on your feet. But in the end, even the act of moving on... is one of life's greatest challenges, beat.

I wondered what kind of poem I would write the next day. And couldn't help but smile a small, gentle smile.

About The Author

Roan McAuley is a contributing author to the Storyshares library.

About The Publisher

Story Shares is a nonprofit focused on supporting the millions of teens and adults who struggle with reading by creating a new shelf in the library specifically for them. The ever-growing collection features content that is compelling and culturally relevant for teens and adults, yet still readable at a range of lower reading levels.

Story Shares generates content by engaging deeply with writers, bringing together a community to create this new kind of book. With more intriguing and approachable stories to choose from, the teens and adults who have fallen behind are improving their skills and beginning to discover the joy of reading. For more information, visit storyshares.org.

Easy to Read. Hard to Put Down.

The Sapling

www.ingramcontent.com/pod-product-compliance
Lightning Source LLC
Chambersburg PA
CBHW071225170626
46809CB00005BA/1938